Charles M. Schulz

Good Grief!
Gardening Is Hard
Work!

HarperHorizon
An Imprint of HarperCollins*Publishers*

First published in 1999 by HarperCollins*Publishers* Inc.
http://www.harpercollins.com

http://www.snoopy.com
ISBN 0-694-01049-9
Printed in China

"As soon as this ground is spaded, I'm going to organize my garden. I'm going to plant potatoes, and beans, and radishes and peas."

"Why are you telling me all this?"

"Just dump me by the side of the road."

"I need someone to help me spade my garden."

Here's the world famous hired hand ready to go to work . . .

"Okay, hired hand ... Here's what I want you to do ... I need this whole yard spaded so I can plant my garden ... Are you sure you've done this kind of work before?"

"The phone's ringing . . . I'll be out in
a minute to show you what to do . . ."

"I'm sorry, I can't talk to you now . . . My hired hand and I are planting my garden . . ."

"Okay, hired hand, let's start planting my garden . . ."

"Where are all the seeds? Don't tell me you've planted them already? Boy, you'r[e] some hard worker! Well, all we have to [do] now is wait for everything to come up! "